Donald made a fire in the backyard,
and they all roasted hot dogs over it.

"This is great," said Huey.

"It's the best," said Dewey.

"Pass the ketchup," said Louie.

"You see," said Donald.
"Nothing bad lasts forever.
Our bad day has turned out
just fine."

The boys changed
out of their wet
things...

and gave them to
Donald to hang
on the line.

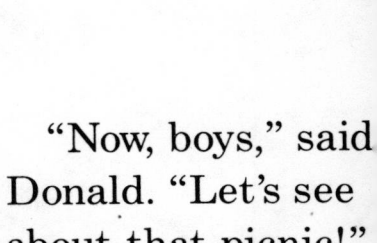

"Now, boys," said
Donald. "Let's see
about that picnic!"

Donald and the boys felt the warm sun. "Hey!" said Donald. "The day is not over yet. We can still have a picnic!"

At last Donald and the boys got home.
They all felt miserable.
Suddenly the sun broke through the clouds.
"Look!" said Huey. "The storm is over!"

Donald and the boys drove home in the rain.
They were cold, wet, and hungry.
"This has been a BAD day!" said Donald.

At last the car moved forward.
Donald stopped to let the boys in.
"Oh, NO-O!" said Donald when he saw them.
The boys were covered with mud.

Huey, Dewey, and Louie got out of the car.
They tried to push it forward.
Donald pressed hard on the gas pedal.
The wheels spun around and around.
Mud splattered all over.

But Donald's troubles were STILL not over.
Now his car was stuck in the mud.

Donald held
up a soggy bag.
"You can't
eat these
sandwiches,"
he said.

Huey let the water out of the car.
"Come on, boys," said Donald.
"There's nothing to do but go home."

But Donald's troubles were not over.
The car was full of rain water.
"Oh, no!" said Donald. "The lunch bags
are soaking wet!"

"Uncle Donald, we're hungry," said the boys. "We don't have any lunch."

"I know. Your sandwiches are in the car," said Donald. "Let's go and get them."

He led the boys back to his car.

Donald heard the boys quarreling.
He followed the sound of their voices.
"Hello, boys," said Donald. "Have you
seen Daisy?"
"She's with Gladstone Gander," said
Huey. "I think he's taking her home."
"Humph," said Donald. "She could
have left me a note."

"Uncle Donald forgot to pack lunch for us!" said Huey.

"Why didn't you check the knapsacks before we left?" said Dewey.

"Why didn't YOU?" said Louie.

"It's not MY fault!" said Huey.

The boys found a dry spot.
"Let's sit here and have lunch," said Huey.
"Good idea," said Louie. "I'm starved."
The boys opened their knapsacks.
"Hey, there's no lunch!" said Dewey.

Not far away Huey, Dewey, and Louie were also caught in the rain.

They decided to wait under the trees until the rain stopped.

As the boys walked into the woods, they saw Daisy and Gladstone passing by.

"I bet she went into
the woods," said Donald.
"It's dryer under the trees."
    So Donald went into
the woods to look for Daisy.

And Donald did get soaked.

He was very unhappy.

At last he got back to his car with the water.

"Oh, no!" he said. "Where's Daisy?"

So Daisy drove off with
Gladstone.

"Donald will get soaked,"
she said. "Serves him right!"

Along came a friend—Gladstone Gander.

"What are you doing here?" he asked.

"Getting wet," said Daisy. "And it's all Donald's fault."

"Want a lift?" asked Gladstone.

"You bet," said Daisy. "Want to share a picnic lunch when we get home?"

Suddenly it began to rain.

"Oh, no," said Daisy. "Now what am
I supposed to do?"

Donald set off to find some water.
He hoped he did not have far to go.

Donald walked
and walked.
Clouds began to
pile up in the sky.

Donald kept
walking.
He felt very hot.

The day grew hotter and hotter.
So did the water in Donald's car.
Suddenly the radiator cap flew off.
BAM-HSSsss! The water steamed out.
"Oh, dear," said Daisy.
"Oh, rats," said Donald.

"Don't you think you should have the top on your car?" asked Daisy. "The weather is so hot. We might get a sudden storm."

"No, it won't rain," said Donald. "I can always tell. Trust me."

And off they drove.

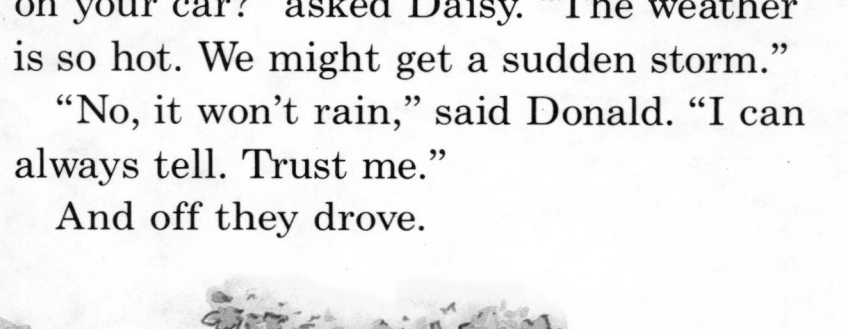

Daisy was waiting for Donald.
"Yoo-hoo, Donald," she called.
"Look, I've packed lunch for us."
"Great!" said Donald.
Daisy's lunches were the best.

Donald put the sandwiches
in his car.
Then he looked up at the sky.
He saw only a few clouds.
"I don't think it will rain,"
he said. "I won't take the top
to my car."

Donald looked
at the clock.

"Wow!" he said. "I'd better hurry up
or I'll be late for my date with Daisy."

On the way out Donald picked up
the boys' lunches.

"I might as well
take these," he said.
"Maybe I'll see the
boys along the way."

"Oh, no!" said Donald when he got inside.
The breakfast was burning on the stove.
The boys had eaten only cereal.
And they had left their lunch bags behind.
They had not noticed that their knapsacks
were empty.

Donald went back to fixing the fence.
He tried to hit a nail with his hammer.
But he hit his finger instead.
"Yee-OWW!" he yelled.

He dashed indoors
to run cool water
on his finger.

Donald began to fix the fence.

Huey, Dewey, and Louie came outside.

They were wearing their knapsacks.

"We're off on our hike," said Huey.

"Wait, boys," said Donald. "You haven't had your breakfast!"

"Yes, we have," said Dewey.

"So long," said Louie.

And off they went.

Donald looked sadly at his garden.
"That rabbit ate a lot," he said.
"I'd better fix the fence before he
comes back."
So Donald got his tools.

Donald rushed out of the house.
"Get out of here, rabbit!" he yelled.
The rabbit dived through a hole in
the fence and ran away.

Donald began
to cook breakfast.
Then he looked
out the window.
What he saw
made him mad.
A rabbit was
eating his carrots!

The clock chimed
eight.
"Time for the boys
to get up," said
Donald.

"Rise and shine, boys," said Donald.
Huey, Dewey, and Louie groaned.
Then they remembered their hike.
They jumped out of bed.

One morning Donald Duck got up early.
It was going to be a busy day.
He was taking Daisy for a drive in
the country.
And Donald's nephews were going on
a hike for the whole day.
So Donald made sandwiches for their lunch.

WALT DISNEY PRODUCTIONS
presents

Donald Duck's
Bad Day

Random House  **New York**